Crocodile Finds a Home
Produced by IMP Books AB for IKEA FAMILY
Illustrations: Silke Leffler
Text: Karin Salmson
Artwork: Pierre Österholm
Translation Comactiva Translations AB
ISBN 978-91-7417-015-3 US
Printed in Belgium 2008

FABLER

text by Karin Salmson

Crocodile finds a home

illustrated by Silke Leffler

It is a dark, stormy night. The trees are swaying in the wind, and all the
animals are sheltering from the nasty weather.
But SOMEBODY is out.
Two eyes shine in the darkness.
Under a tree, there is something that looks like a log. Well, a log with eyes.
And legs. And a big mouth, full of razor-sharp teeth.

But nobody can see her, because nobody else wants to be outside in the cold
and rain. In fact, Crocodile really doesn't either.
"I wish I had packed my umbrella," thinks Crocodile, using her backpack
as a pillow.
"I suppose I had better try to get some sleep anyway."

When morning comes the storm has calmed down, and sunbeams start finding their way beneath the tree where Crocodile is hiding. She wakes up when she feels the warmth on her nose.
But Crocodile is sneezing, and she's freezing!
"Oh dear, I seem to have caught a cold," she mumbles worriedly.

As Crocodile and the sun wake up, the rest of the forest wakes up too. Not far away, Giraffe is doing his morning exercises.
"And stretch!" shouts Giraffe.
"And down!"
Lying next to Giraffe is someone yawning drowsily. Leopard is certainly not doing any exercises. He's lying there with a carrot in his mouth, reading a book.
"Stretching? No thanks, I'll leave all the stretching to you!" he says to Giraffe.

Crocodile hears their voices, and says to herself:
"I need to get some help with this cold. I will have to find somewhere to live."

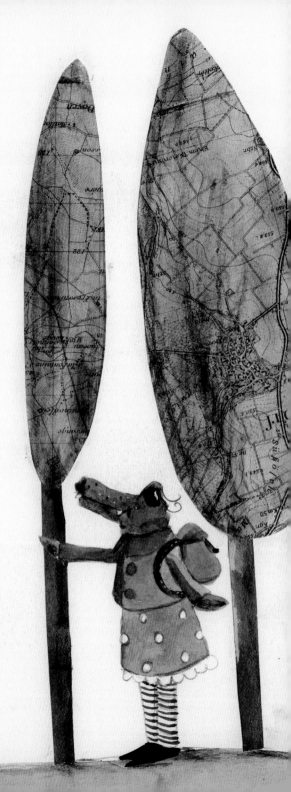

"Hello," says Crocodile, walking into the glade where Giraffe and Leopard live.
"Help!" screams Giraffe, nearly jumping out of his skin.
"Quick! Get up! Run!" he bellows to Leopard, who doesn't take his eyes
off his book.
"Look, I said I don't want to do any exercises," mumbles Leopard.
But then he looks up!
That certainly gets him moving! Like a shot, Leopard runs past Giraffe,
and as they disappear into the forest Crocodile barely manages to say:
"But I only wanted your help…"
But they don't hear her. All they could see was Crocodile's big
mouth with all those razor-sharp teeth.

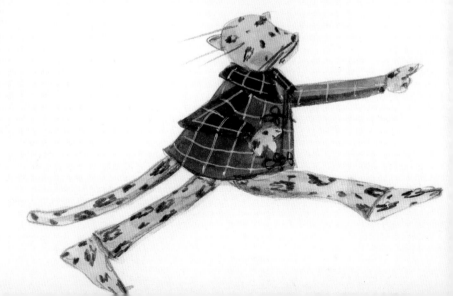

Crocodile sighs. She had heard this village was a lovely, friendly place with a forest, water and meadows to run around in. After all, that was why she had made the long journey to get here. Away from all the other crocodiles who thought she was so odd, because she only wanted to eat sand cookies.

"But I think this house is too far away from the sand, the beach and all the sand cookies," says Crocodile to nobody but her rumbling tummy.

Crocodile walks on over a small hill and is
pleased to see more little houses. And best
of all, she spots a beach too!
"How nice it would be if I could find someone who needs a roommate!"
Even though she has a bit of a temperature,
she hurries down the hill towards the village.
"Maybe this someone has handkerchiefs,
warm covers and a nice, comforting voice."

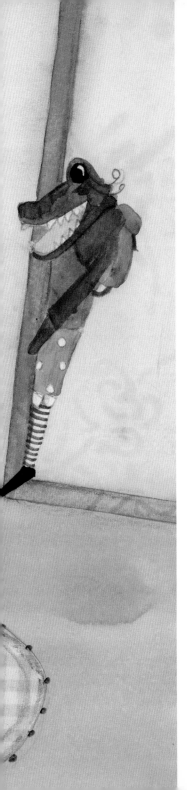

At that very moment, Lion is serving breakfast. Duck, who is a cheerful morning person, gives Lion a good morning kiss. Mouse and Cow, who are nearly always up to mischief, are sitting under the table singing pirate songs.

"Sit down now and I'll give you extra-special pancakes," says Lion as kindly as he can, which isn't that easy when you have a rumbling lion's voice.

"Ahem, hello?" says Crocodile, standing in the doorway. "Don't be scared!" she adds quickly.

"He… he… heeelp!" screams Lion, dropping the frying pan on the floor with a crash, and flying up into Duck's arms.

"Lion's singing!" Cow giggles.

"Yeah, yeah, yeah!" Mouse adds happily.

"Silence!" hisses Duck, suddenly in not such a good morning mood.

"Who are you?! What do you want?!" she says roughly to Crocodile.

"Uh, my name's Crocodile," answers Crocodile, trying to look as harmless as possible, which isn't easy when you have lovely sharp teeth like Crocodile (with no fillings!).

"I am looking for a place where I can rest, or perhaps even live," says Crocodile with a doubtful voice. Just then, she sneezes.

Lion has now climbed down from Duck. Not that he had much choice. As Duck would tell him later, ducks don't have very strong wings.

"Here you go," he says, carefully holding out a handkerchief.

"You seem to have a cold."

"Well, as I'm sure you can see, we already have a full house!" says Duck irritably.

"You will have to look somewhere else. And don't go frightening good, decent people at this time of the morning!"

Crocodile backs out of the door.

"Well, thanks anyway," she says, and walks off.

"A crocodile, here, in our quiet little village? That simply won't do! Walking around with teeth like razors!" mutters Duck, helping herself to pancakes.

"Oh well, at least I have a hanky," says Crocodile.

"Is it even worth asking in another house?" she sighs.

Just then, Leopard rushes past with a big swooosh!

"Oh!" Crocodile exclaims, as Leopard vanishes into the house in front of her.

The door slams with a loud bang!

Before she even has time to catch her breath, swoosh – bang! again as Giraffe gallops past screaming, "Heeeeeeelp!"

They were in such a hurry they never even saw Crocodile.

The house window is open, and Crocodile can't help herself stepping closer so she can hear what they're saying.

"It's true! A crocodile! It wanted to eat us up!"

Crocodile peeks up through the window. Leopard has been talking, and Giraffe adds:

"It was chasing us, but I think we got away. But we can never go back to our house now! We've been driven away!"

"Are you sure about this?" asks Bear, looking troubled.

Giraffe and Leopard nod excitedly.

"And we have so much to do today. This could ruin everything!" growls Bear.

Crocodile's heart sinks like a stone. A tear rolls down her cheek. Now she will have to keep on wandering. Will she ever find a place where she is welcome?

"But I've got a cold," she whispers with a sniff.

Just then, she hears a hullabaloo from the square she has just passed.

"What's going on?" she wonders anxiously.

"Moouuse!" shouts Duck.

"We're losing him!" screams Lion.

"Help!" moos Cow.

Mouse, rising up into the sky, gives a little squeak.

"I'll jump," yells Giraffe as he comes rushing along.

Everyone holds their breath as Giraffe gets a big running start and jumps up towards Mouse.

But it's not high enough!

"I can't look!" says Leopard, hiding his eyes in his paws.

"Where's Frog?!" calls Bear desperately.

"I'm coming! Goodness me! What powerful gas you must have in those balloons!" says Frog, as she gathers speed and jumps up towards Mouse.

"Nearly!" she says, as she comes back down to earth again. Meanwhile Crocodile has joined the animals, but nobody has noticed her. They are all looking up at Mouse.

Frog leaps up again and just manages to grab the string Mouse is hanging from.

"Hooray!" the animals shout.

But the danger is not over yet!

"I'm too light! I'm only coming halfway down. I can't bring Mouse down, and I can't untangle him either!" hollers Frog.

"Giraffe, you can reach me! Bite the string!"

But Giraffe's teeth are not strong enough.

Lion starts to cry:

"Save our Mouse!"

Then Crocodile stands on tiptoe and stretches her long mouth up to the string.

"Help!" shouts Giraffe terrified, and leaps out of the way.

Crocodile bites the string, and as the balloon floats up into the sky, Crocodile catches Mouse in her arms.

"Wow – what great teeth you have!" says Frog with admiration, having landed gracefully back down to earth again.

"Thanks," says Crocodile, smiling.

Duck rushes up to Crocodile and gives her a big hug. Her good morning mood is back.

"Oh, careful, I have a cold! I don't want you to catch it," says Crocodile, blushing.

"I'm not worried about that!" laughs Duck.

"Is this that dangerous Crocodile you were talking about?"

asks Bear, glaring at Leopard.

"Yes, well… I thought… she looked dangerous…

but maybe not…," stutters Leopard, also blushing now.

Frog puts out her hand to Crocodile.

"My name's Frog. What's yours?"

"Crocodile," says Crocodile.

"This is Bear, Leopard, Duck, Lion, Mouse, Cow and Giraffe,"
says Frog, pointing to each of her friends in turn.

"And we'd really like you to come to my birthday party today!"

"Ooh yes, come, please do!" says Giraffe.

And of course, Crocodile would love to come!

But: "Ah-choo!!"

"Hmm, that doesn't sound very good," says Bear. "Come with me
and I'll get you some nice refreshing tea."

"Then you can come to my house and have a rest
while we get everything ready for the party,"
suggests Frog.

Before they set off, Duck suddenly adds:

"Just think! What luck that you just happened to
be passing, with your sharp teeth and everything.
Do you know what? I don't even have teeth!"

In bed back at Frog's house, Crocodile lies there, thinking. She thinks about how lucky it was that she was brave enough to jump in and help – otherwise Mouse would have been carried away by the balloon! She couldnt bear thinking about it! Mouse could have vanished forever and might never have found his way home. He might have had to wander around looking for a new place to call home. Just like Crocodile.

Just before falling asleep, Crocodile mumbles:

"Oh well, at least I'm going to a party before I carry on looking!"

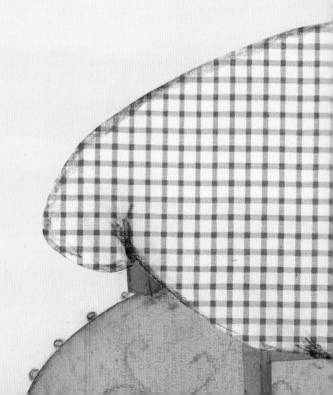

When Frog wakes Crocodile up, she is feeling much, much better. And now everybody is sitting around the party table. All the presents have been opened, and everyone has had lots of nice food and drink.

"I'm sorry I didn't have a present for you," says Crocodile.

"But you did! You helped me save Mouse!" says Frog with a smile.

But then Frog suddenly looks a bit sad.

"What's the matter?" wonders Crocodile, concerned.

"Oh, it's nothing," replies Frog.

"Do you know what?" says Crocodile.

"I've noticed that if you have friends around you, if you have people who want to listen to you, you should tell them what's the matter."

Frog looks at Crocodile, and then she says:

"It's just that sometimes I feel lonely. I love the water and the beach and, well, sometimes I'd like to have someone to share it with. Duck nearly always seems to think the water's too cold to go for a swim. Do you see what I mean?"

Crocodile nods.

Of course she sees. She pats Frog on the cheek.

And that's when it HAPPENS.

THAT'S when Frog says:

"I know it's a funny thing to ask for on your birthday… but I would really like you to stay with me."

Crocodile could not be happier. With a big smile she shows all her lovely teeth and squeals:

"Oh, YES! Oh, I'd love to! I love water, and I love this place! And I love it that you wanted me to come to your party! I really would love to stay if you'll let me!"

And so Crocodile found a home. She found Frog's home, and Frog found someone to take away her loneliness and share her love of the water and they love taking a dip together, making sand cookies, or even putting on a show that the others can watch (even though some of them might sometimes prefer not to).

And that was how they all came to live happily ever after.

THE END

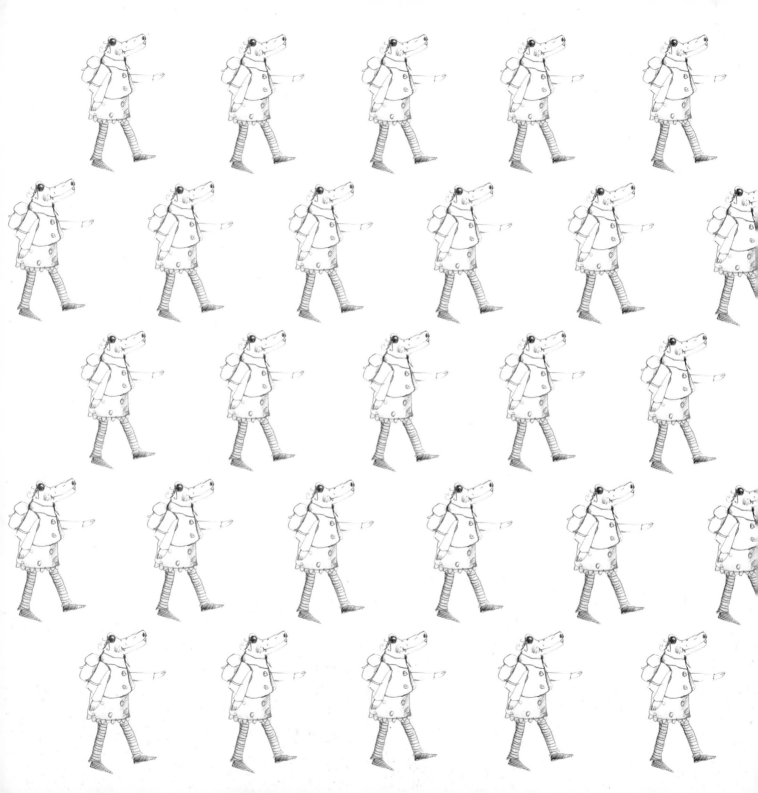